Don't Spoil Y
The Body Book

Claire Rayner

Introduction by Dr. Richard Lansdown
Illustrated by Tony King

BARRON'S

New York

First edition for the United States published 1989 by
Barron's Educational Series, Inc.

First published 1989 by The Bodley Head Ltd., London, England.

All inquiries should be addressed to:
Barron's Educational Series, Inc.
250 Wireless Boulevard, Hauppauge, New York 11788

Library of Congress Catalog Card No. 89-143

International Standard Book No. 0-8120-6098-9

Library of Congress Cataloging-in-Publication Data
Rayner, Claire.
The don't spoil your body book/Claire Rayner; introduction by Richard Lansdown; illustrated by Tony King.—1st ed.
p.   cm.
Summary: Explains physiological effects of drugs, including alcohol and tobacco, making clear precisely how each
substance harms the body and undermines its performance.
ISBN 0-8120-6098-9
1. substance abuse—Physiological aspects—Juvenile literature.
[1. Drug Abuse.] I. King, Tony, 1947– ill. II. Title. III. Title: Body book.
RC564.R39 1989
616.86—dc19   89–143
                               CIP
                               AC

PRINTED IN ITALY
9012   987654321

Contents

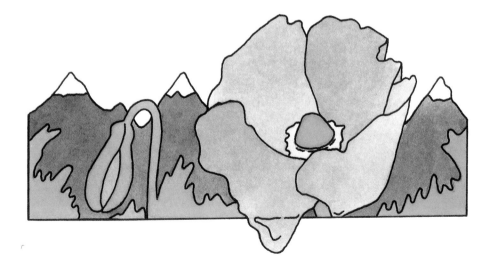

Foreword

It was indeed a pleasure to read this book. I found it well-written, informative, and medically accurate. It has many valuable lessons to teach the intended audience.

The audience which is most likely to profit from this book would be parents who are looking for information about substance abuse to share with their adolescents and pre-adolescents. The book is certainly written so that even a ten year old could read and comprehend most of the material. Younger children would need adult backup both for discussion and explanation of facts. The figures graphically illustrate the messages of the accompanying text and will appeal to and will hold the atttention of children.

There's a lot of drug information around, but not much especially wrtitten for children. This book fills that gap.

Willam Sears, MD,FRCP
San Clemente, California

Introduction

It is so easy to underestimate children, to think that because they are young they understand only what is immediately in front of them. It is so easy to assume that children should be shielded from painful thoughts, of illness and death for example, because such ideas are beyond them and because childhood is, or should be, an age of innocence.

Well, yes, childhood innocence is precious and we shatter it at our peril. But children should be taught something of the world that is awaiting them, so that they are better prepared to cope with it. If, while they are still young, they can learn of some of the possible pains and dangers to which they may be tempted as they grow up, they are more likely to be in a position to hold out against the pressures that will inevitably come.

On the other hand, children have only a limited range of thought processes and experience to bring to bear on topics like those discussed in this book. So anything written for them has to be not only straightforward in its language, it has to get across complex ideas in a simple way. This is where Claire Rayner and Tony King have succeeded: they offer a message that pulls no punches, that includes some of the most important topics that face young people today and yet is coached in a way that keeps a young child's understanding in mind.

There is one further plus to this book and that is its positive ending. So much health education carries a message only of impending dangers and of the need constantly to avoid them. The trouble with this approach is that it offers nothing in the place of temptation. *The Don't Spoil Your Body Book* offers more than that; it includes positive ideas on how to get excitement from life in ways that are not only healthy but fun as well.

I enjoyed reading it and I am sure that it will be of enormous help to many children, now and in the future.

Richard Lansdown, PhD
Chief Psychologist
The Hospital for Sick Children
London, England

5

Your Good Body

Your body is very clever. It knows the things it has to do without your telling it, or thinking about it.

You don't have to tell your teeth how to chew, or your throat how to swallow.

You don't have to tell your stomach how to digest your food, or your intestines how to send your food to all the different parts of you to be made into you.

You don't have to tell your muscles how to work, or your joints how to bend, or your eyes how to see, or your ears how to hear.

All these things, and many, many more, your body does by itself because it is so very clever.

All your body's different parts are clever on their own, but they are even more clever than that. They also know how to work together with each other so that all of you will be comfortable.

And healthy.

And happy.

Look at what happens when you eat, for example.

Your stomach is empty, so it sends a message to your brain to say, "I am empty!"

Your brain then sends a message to the

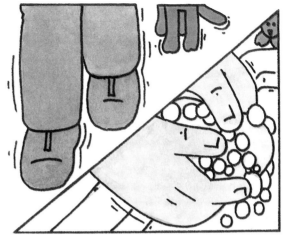

rest of your body to say, "It's dinner time. Go and eat your dinner, so that your stomach is not empty anymore."

Your legs then walk to the bathroom to wash your hands—and to the dining room to sit down—and then they bend at the knees and hips so that you can sit down.

Your eyes see the food on the table. It looks good and that makes your brain send a message to your stomach to say, "the food is coming soon!" And your stomach gets so excited it squeezes itself, and you feel the squeezing and know how hungry you are.

Your nose smells the food on the table. It smells good and your brain sends a message

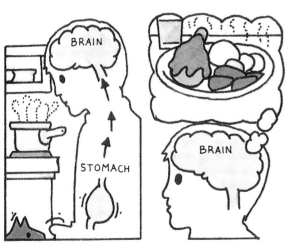

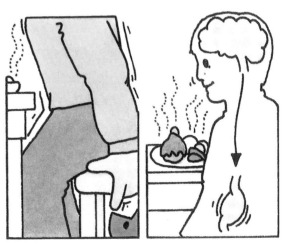

to your mouth to say, "The food is coming soon! Get ready to soften it and chew it and send it to the waiting stomach." And your mouth begins to make more saliva, so you swallow and that makes your stomach get excited again and squeeze itself. And you feel the squeezing and know how *very* hungry you are.

Now your food is in front of you, and your brain gets very busy, telling all the different parts of you what to do and when to do it.

And all the parts of you do different things all at the same time.

Your arms move your hands so that you pick up your knife and fork. Your hands move so that you cut up the food. Your arms carry the food to your mouth and put it in. You start to chew with your teeth while your tongue tastes the food and moves it around your mouth to make sure all the different bits are chewed up.

Your gullet carries the food down to your stomach, which starts to squeeze and churn, churn and squeeze, so that the food is broken up small enough to go into your intestine and then be sent all over your body in your blood to make new bits of your body.

And all the time you are doing all these things and enjoying them, you can talk and listen and look as your voice and your ears and your eyes are working too. And your lungs are breathing air in and out and your heart is beating so that your blood travels all over your body to do its work, and all the different parts of you are quietly getting on with the work of being your clever body.

It is like a great orchestra of lots of different instruments, all making beautiful music together.

But what happens if some of the parts of your body aren't allowed to work as they should? That can make the whole body work badly. Just as when an instrument in an orchestra plays badly, then the music stops being beautiful, and is spoiled.

Bodies, too, can be spoiled.

Smoke and Your Body

You know about smoking. You've seen the advertisements for cigarettes on posters and in newspapers and magazines. You've seen the advertisements for pipes and cigars on television. And you've seen grown ups smoking.

Why do they do it?

For most grown-ups who smoke, it is a habit. They started smoking one day, and then found it hard to stop.

And that is very sad, because there are things in tobacco that spoil your body badly.

Your body stops being so clever. It stops being able to do some of the things it is supposed to do.

Why, then, do people start to smoke?

Sometimes it is because someone else dares them to.

Or because they see other people doing it.

Or because they think it is a grown-up thing to do.

Or because they believe the advertisements, which pretend that smoking is all fun and doesn't really hurt you much.

(Well, the advertisements would say that, wouldn't they? The people who grow the tobacco and who make the cigarettes and the cigars and pipes do it to make money. So they won't tell the truth about tobacco on their posters, will they?)

What is the truth about smoking?

Smoke is not just a gray cloud. It is made up of very tiny scraps of solid stuff.

Some of it is called NICOTINE.

Some of it is called TAR.

Some of it is a gas called CARBON MONOXIDE.

Some of it is called AMMONIA.

And some of it is made up of a thousand other chemicals!

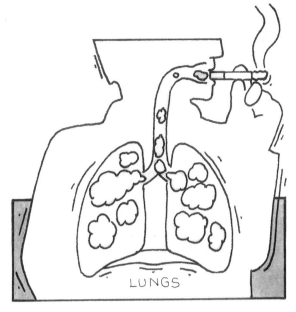

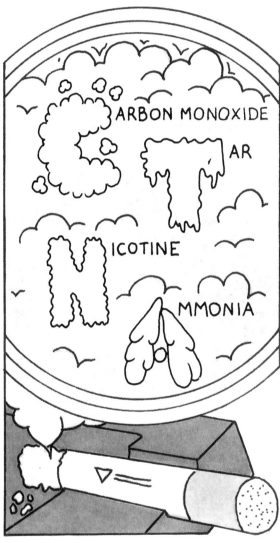

The NICOTINE in cigarette smoke does unpleasant and dangerous things inside your body.

It gets into your lungs.

Then it gets into your blood and travels all over your body when your heart beats to push the blood along the blood vessels.

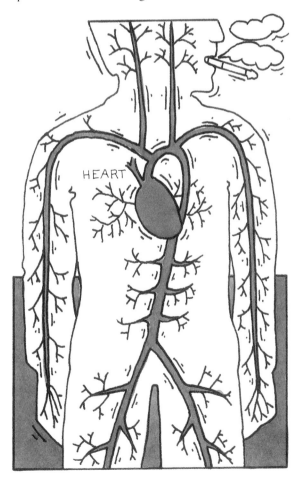

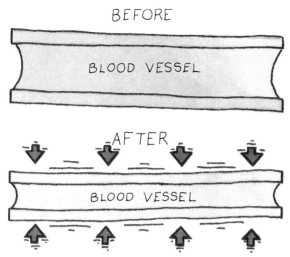

BEFORE

BLOOD VESSEL

AFTER

BLOOD VESSEL

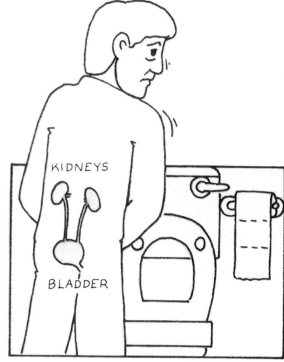

KIDNEYS

BLADDER

It makes muscles go tight. This makes the blood vessels get narrower, because their walls are made of muscles.

It makes the heart beat faster to push the blood along the narrow vessels. So it has to work much harder.

It makes the blood press harder on the walls of the blood vessels (not surprisingly this is called blood pressure!), and that means all sorts of other body parts have to work harder too.

And your nerves. They have the important job of carrying messages around your body to tell it what to do and how to feel.

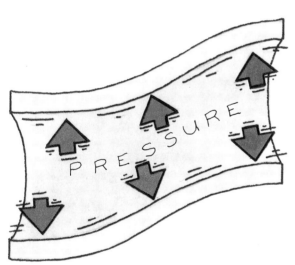

PRESSURE

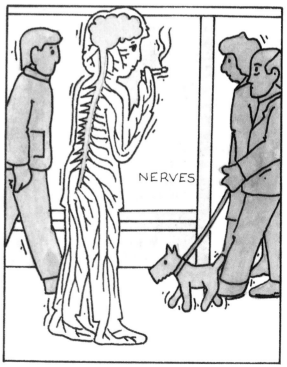

NERVES

Like your kidneys. They have the important job of getting rid of wastes from your food and drink, by making urine—the water that comes out of your body when you urinate.

RED BLOOD CELLS

PLATELETS

And your blood. This has the important job of carrying the food and water you swallow and the oxygen you breathe in around your body. When nicotine gets into blood, it makes some of the cells sticky, and they clump together, sticking to the walls of the blood vessels. This makes the blood vessels even narrower, and the heart and kidneys have to work harder than ever.

Sometimes the heart just can't get enough blood from the narrow blood vessels and the result is called a heart attack. The heart is damaged and sometimes the person dies.

This is very sad and such a silly waste if it happens because of smoking tobacco with nicotine in it.

TAR in cigarette smoke does unpleasant things inside your body.

It is thick, brown, sticky stuff, and each puff of cigarette smoke is full of tiny, tiny bits of it. They are so small you could get ten thousand onto a pinhead, which is why you can't see them. When people smoke a cigarette they take in a million million tar droplets. When they breathe out, almost three quarters of that million million droplets stay inside their lungs. Inside the lungs the tar feels dreadful. It irritates, and that makes the smoker cough. And because of the nicotine in the smoke the muscular tubes they cough through are made narrower, so coughing is very difficult. That is why when some smokers cough they get very red and their blood vessels swell on their faces and in their necks as they struggle to get enough

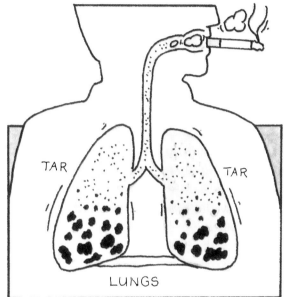

TAR   TAR

LUNGS

tarry mess out of their lungs to let air in.

There is something else that makes it hard for smokers to cough out the tar they have

breathed in. Inside the lungs, all the tubes are lined with tiny, tiny hairs called cilia. These have the job of being brooms. They wave about, and when unwanted stuff is breathed in—like dust from the floor and pollen from the flowers and germs that cause illnesses—they sweep it right out again.

But when smokers breathe in tar, the little hairs are paralyzed. They can't wave about

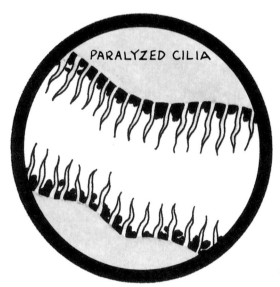

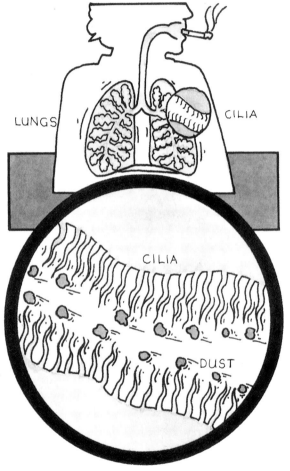

There is something else that tar does, which is worse than disgusting. It is extremely dangerous.

anymore and do their important job. So the tar stays there. And stays there. And stays there and stays there . . . .

And so the smokers have very clogged, dirty lungs and get more colds and illnesses than they would have had.

They have to cough a lot to try to get rid of all the mess in their lungs. Then they have to spit it out. Isn't that disgusting?

Because the tar irritates the tender soft lining of the lungs, it hurts the cells that make up the lining. Hurt cells stop growing as they should. They grow the wrong shape and they grow too much. They grow and they grow and they make a disease called cancer.

Cancer in the lungs and in the throat, which is where the tar in cigarette smoke makes most cancers, is a very dangerous type. It is not easy to cure.

16

Most of the people who get cancer in these parts of their bodies die. Their bodies have been completely spoiled.

The CARBON MONOXIDE in cigarette smoke also does some very unpleasant

things inside your body.

It stops your blood from carrying enough oxygen around by getting into the blood cells where the oxygen ought to be.

Then the muscles can't do their work properly and the liver can't do its work properly and none of the body can do its work properly.

If a woman who smokes had a baby inside her, trying to grow big enough to be born, then the baby will be given all the things that are in the smoke.

The nicotine will make its blood vessels tight, and its heart overworked, and the carbon monoxide will stop the oxygen getting to its muscles and kidneys and other important parts.

And then the baby can't grow.

Sometimes the baby is so starved of the good things it ought to get from its mother's blood, like food and oxygen, and gets so much of the things it shouldn't have, like nicotine and carbon monoxide, that it can't

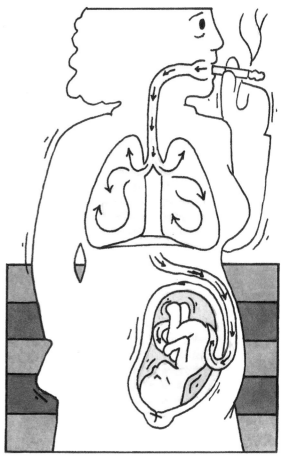

grow big. When this happens the baby is born smaller than it ought to be.

And that makes it hard for the baby to grow up as healthy as it could be.

Sometimes it can't grow up at all, and may even die.

So a smoking mother not only spoils her own clever body. She spoils her baby's clever body as well.

The AMMONIA, and the thousand other things that are in cigarette smoke, do the same sorts of things to smokers' bodies. They make each and every part of them less well, just as the whole orchestra sounds wrong when one of the instruments isn't playing as it should.

And it isn't only tobacco smoke that does all these bad things.

Some people sniff powdered tobacco called snuff. This irritates the soft nasal tissue and makes people sneeze.

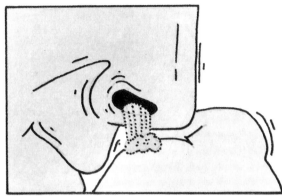

Some people suck chopped tobacco inside little bags like tea bags. This is called wet snuff.

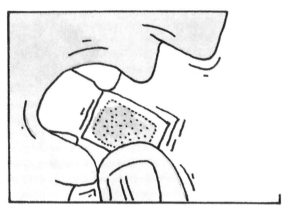

Some people chew tobacco.

But whether tobacco is chewed, sucked, sniffed, or smoked, it puts dangerous disgusting things into people's bodies.

It spoils the taste of their food. It makes them more likely to be ill. It makes them very unpleasant to be with.

People who use tobacco smell nasty. Their breath, their clothes, everything about them smells stale and nasty.

Their teeth look yellow and dull.

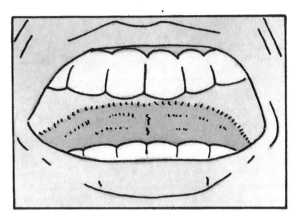

Their fingers may look yellow, too.

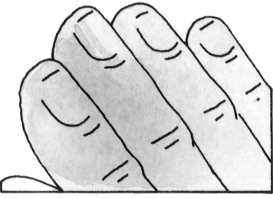

They don't look at all like people with good clever bodies.

So why do people use tobacco when it does such bad things to them?

Not all the bad things that smoke does feel bad. When nicotine and carbon monoxide get into the brain, for example, they make some parts of it seem to work faster.

So the person who smokes feels a bit more alert and lively for a very little while.

Nicotine and carbon monoxide also make some parts of the brain seem to work slower.

So the person who smokes feels a bit more relaxed and peaceful for a little time.

But these feelings don't last. To get them again, the smoker needs more and more smoke. And more, and more and more . . . .

So, though the first puff of tobacco smoke, or the first taste of snuff, may make people feel sick and giddy and sweaty, if they go on trying it, some of the bad feelings seem less, as they get used to them, and some of the good feelings feel better.

But eventually there are neither especially good feelings nor especially bad ones. These people have just gotten used to smok-

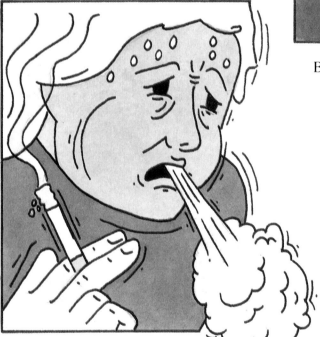

ing and go on doing it. They feel they can't do without it, because when they stop, the bad feelings come rushing back. They feel miserable and twitchy and sick and very, very bad tempered.

That is why it is so hard to give up the habit once it has started.

Better not to start at all, don't you agree?

Chemical Smells and Your Body

Here is glue.

Here is hair spray.

Here are gasoline and paint, nail polish and clothes cleaner, lighter fuel and antifreeze for cars.

All these different things are used for different jobs. But there is something that is the same about all of them. They smell very strong.

This is because they have in them special chemicals, which are *volatile*. That means that like little birds they fly up out of their container into the air in tiny, tiny droplets. It is the droplets that carry the strong smell.

But the droplets are more than just a strong smell. They can get into people's noses and mouths, and then into their lungs. Once they are there they can get into the blood, and go all over the body, especially to the brain.

When the chemicals in the droplets get to the brain, they make the cells there behave strangely.

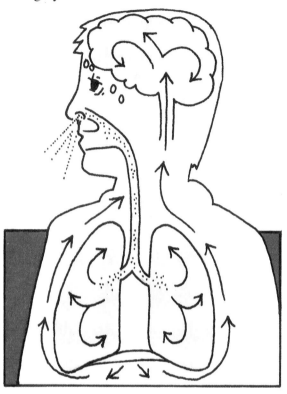

The cells, which help you to see, stop seeing straight so everything looks fuzzy.

The cells, which tell you that you are standing up, stop holding you firm so that you wobble about.

The cells, which tell your tongue and voice how to speak, stop sending the right messages so your speech becomes slurred and silly.

JAK 'N' JILL
WEN' UB A 'ILL

And the cells, which send messages to your heart and lungs and all other parts,

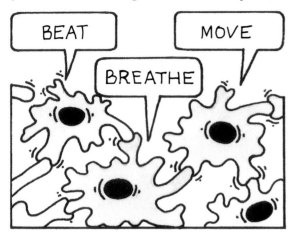

telling them the work they have to do, can't do their job properly, so your heart beats much harder and your lungs breathe much faster, and all the orchestra of your body goes out of tune and time.

You would think that sensible people would not like to have this happen to them, so they would make sure they didn't breathe in droplets from chemicals.

Most people are sensible and they do make sure. But there are some people who like the strange feelings that come from breathing in these volatile droplets.

Maybe they are bored.
Or miserable.
Or lonely.

Maybe they see someone else breathing these chemicals and think it's what people are supposed to do, so they copy them.

Maybe someone dares them to.
And so they do it.
Sometimes it makes them very sick. Sometimes it gives them bad pains in their bellies. Sometimes they get headaches.

So they never do it again.
They are sensible.

But some people are so bored and miserable and such copycats that they do it again. And this time the bad feelings don't feel quite so bad. And sometimes, though not always, they make the person feel excited— and some people like that.

If all you got from chemical smells was excitement for a little while, it would be all right, wouldn't it?

But chemical smells can spoil your body.

They can spoil some of your brain cells for good so that they can never work properly again.

They can spoil some of your heart muscles for good so that your heart becomes weak and can't do its job of beating as it should.

They can burn the skin round your nose and mouth, where the chemicals touch, and make it sore and spotty.

They can make your nose run all the time so that you look snotty and nasty and no one wants to be with you.

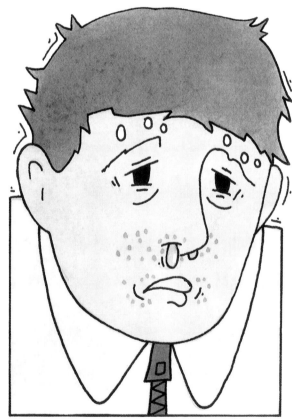

They can make you smell bad, so that people stay away from you more and more.

They can make you feel very sick, and make you be sick—a lot.

They can make you have convulsions—when your whole body starts jerking and you become unconscious and wet yourself.

They can make you feel very miserable and bad tempered and generally horrible.

What do you do if you want to have good feelings but don't want bad ones?

You make sure you never sniff chemicals. All chemicals give you bad feelings and spoil your body.

And you try the different ways there are to feel excited and happy and good without spoiling your body. Look on pages 43–48. That is where you will find the safe ways to feel good.

Alcohol and Your Body

Millions and millions of years ago, even before there were history books, a person somewhere was so hungry that he ate some rotten fruit he found. . . . And that is just how alcohol was discovered.

Alcohol is made when germs that are always in the air start to work on sugar and change it. There is sugar in fruit, so when it gets rotten, the sugar turns into alcohol.

ALCOHOL is a poison. But it is a strange sort of poison.

If you drink a lot of it, you die.

If you drink a little bit of it, you get interesting feelings.

It happens to wasps and bees and animals too if they eat rotten fruit. Have you ever seen wasps fly in a wobbly way over the apples that fell from an apple tree?

They have discovered alcohol just as the prehistoric person did.

He told all his friends and relatives about it and, ever since, people all over the world have used alcohol.

If it only gave people interesting feelings, then that would be all right.

But it does not. It makes some people ill. They are the people who like the feelings so much that they drink more and more alcohol to get more and more of the feelings. But that doesn't work, because you get fewer good feelings from the alcohol as your body gets used to it.

A person who once found he felt happy and giggly and relaxed and comfortable (which are the good feelings) for a long time when he drank one glass of wine, very soon finds he has to drink several glasses to get the good feelings just for a little while.

And the more he drinks, the more he is taking in of the poison that can spoil his body. And that gives him bad feelings.

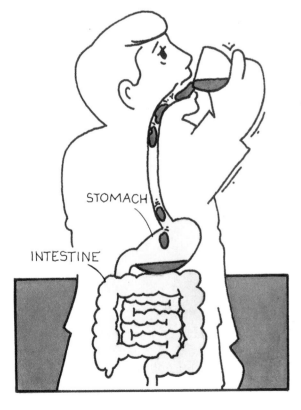

STOMACH

INTESTINE

What does drinking too much alcohol do to a person's body?

It goes into the blood and from there it goes everywhere in the body, just like all the other poisons discussed in this book.

When the alcohol gets to the brain, it makes some of the cells sleepy. This is why alcohol is called a sedative.

The first part of the brain gets sleepy is the one that tells us to behave sensibly instead of being silly, selfish, and cruel.

It is silly to roll around and shout, to sing nasty songs at the top of your voice, and to be rude to people and swear a lot.

It is selfish to make a lot of noise and be sick and urinate in public places.

It is cruel to shout at people and hit them and hurt them.

The next part of your brain that is made sleepy is the part that you think with.

Alcohol makes it so sleepy that people think they can still think properly, even though they can't.

So if they drive a car,

Or use dangerous machinery,

Or try to cross the road safely,

They can't.

Lots of the people hurt or killed in accidents had been drinking alcohol before the accident happened.

These are all the things that some people do when they are drunk from taking too much alcohol.

When the alcohol gets to the liver, it makes it very ill.

The liver is the biggest inside part of you, and it has a very important job. It makes all the poisons that get into you unpoisonous. There are all sorts of small poisons that get into you from ordinary food, and that is why your liver has this job.

But alcohol is a very big poison, and

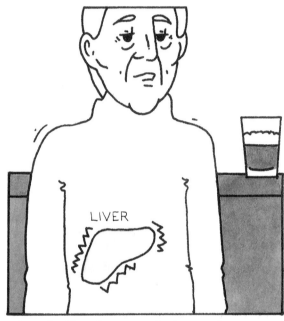

when the liver has to make it unpoisonous, it has to work so hard that some of its cells are so exhausted they die.

And once they are dead, the liver can't do its job properly. People who drink a lot of alcohol often have very ill livers, and that means they can't eat properly.

And they feel sick all the time.

And they turn an ugly yellow color, because the poisons the liver can't get rid of stay in the body and show up in the skin. Having an ill liver is very dangerous.

When the alcohol gets to a person's stomach, it irritates it and makes the inside red and sore.

Sometimes this makes the person sick.

Sometimes it makes the person stop eat-ing, so he or she gets no food to keep the body repairing itself and working properly.

Sometimes it spoils the vitamins in the food the person does manage to eat, so his or her body still can't work as well as it should.

Sometimes it irritates the stomach lining so much that it bleeds, or wears away into a hole, called an ulcer. Having an ulcer is like having a sore *inside* your body.

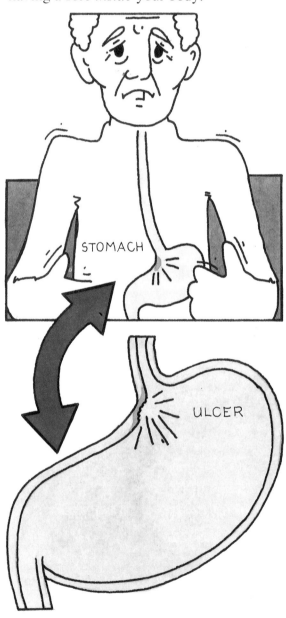

When this happens, the pain can make the person feel very ill indeed, of course.

When the alcohol gets to the kidneys, they know it is a poison, so they try to wash it out by making lots and lots of extra urine.

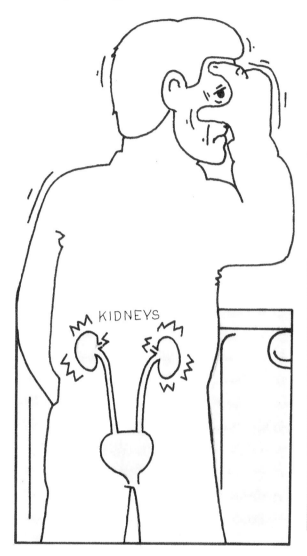

To do that they have to take water from all the body cells. But the body cells need their water to do their work properly. When they can't do their work properly because there isn't enough water in them, then the whole body can't work properly.

Your head aches like a pounding drum.

Your mouth tastes horrible, like the bottom of a dirty birdcage.

Your breath smells disgusting, like the inside of unemptied trash cans.

Your whole body hurts like a punchball that has been hit over and over again.

Your eyes are hot and swollen, sore and become extremely red.

All because you haven't enough water inside the cells of your body!

Other body parts are spoiled when too much alcohol gets to them.

The throat.

The heart.

The nerves.

And all the other parts, too.

If the person who drinks too much alcohol is a woman who is having a baby, then the alcohol goes to the baby too. Sometimes it makes the baby stop growing altogether, so that it dies before it is born.

Sometimes it spoils the baby's brain cells

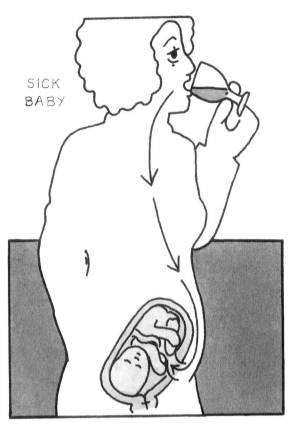

SICK BABY

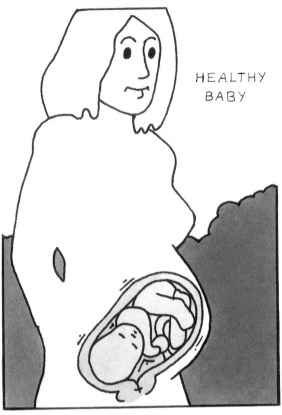

HEALTHY BABY

so that when it is born it is handicapped, and can never grow up to learn properly and to play properly and to have an ordinary life.

It is a very sad thing when a baby has problems from alcohol it didn't drink, but which its mother drank.

Do all people who drink alcohol have spoiled bodies?

No, they do not.

There are lots of people who have a little alcohol sometimes.

They have it to celebrate weddings. Drinking a little champagne, which is bubbly wine which tastes very nice, is fun.

They have it to celebrate the birth of a healthy new baby. It makes everyone—the new mother and father and the new grandmothers and grandfathers and all the relatives and friends—very happy.

Your family probably did it when you were born.

Lots of people have parties and behave sensibly after drinking a little bit of alcohol. And their bodies are clever enough to get rid of that little bit of alcohol without being spoiled!

But some people don't just have a little alcohol for fun.

They have more and more and more and more . . . .

They are the ones who get all the bad effects.

Why do they do it?

No one knows for sure why. Some people may be born with the sort of brain cells that make them want alcohol more than other people do.

They try it once and like it a lot, and then go on and on taking more and more to enjoy the good feelings it gives them.

They even go on taking more and more

after they discover that the good feelings get less and less.

And then they discover after a while that their bodies are so used to alcohol they can't do without it.

If they don't have some, then they feel ill. They don't get good feelings from drinking alcohol anymore. They get bad ones when they don't.

When that has happened, a person is said to be an alcoholic.

That's how people become addicted to alcohol. That means they just can't be comfortable without it.

How can a young person know whether he or she is the sort of person who might become an alcoholic?

When you are very young, you can't know.

Growing from a child into an adult is difficult. You want to be a grown up quickly and do grown-up things, but inside you still feel like a child.

Some young people who are doing their growing-up think they will be more grown-up more quickly if they drink alcohol.

But they are wrong. Being grown-up doesn't come from drinking alcohol. It comes from learning and listening and sharing and from being older.

If you try to use alcohol before you have grown up, it makes growing up harder. It can make young people feel miserable and angry, so they looks for something to take away the bad feelings that come from finding it hard to grow up—and from drinking the alcohol.

Guess what they do then?

They take more alcohol.

And the same thing happens. And they feel bad and takes more alcohol and feels bad and so takes more alcohol . . . .

That is how some people start to be alcoholics.

That is why it is best not to drink alcohol when you are not yet grown-up.

And even when you are, you must remember to drink only a little.

Because alcohol spoils a lot of people's bodies very badly indeed.

Will you ever drink a lot of alcohol?

Drugs and Your Body

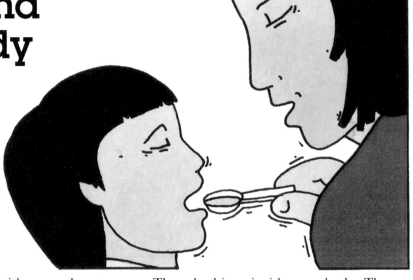

Have you ever been ill with a sore throat or a bad cough or an earache?

Have you every been given some medicine to make you better?

Probably you have. That has happened to everyone at some time or other.

There is another name for the medicines you are given. They are called drugs.

They do things inside your body. These are important things.

Some drugs help keep people well when otherwise they would be ill. Or they help ill people to be more comfortable.

For example, there is an illness called diabetes, which people sometimes died of in the past, but not anymore.

Now they have a drug called insulin, which keeps them alive and well.

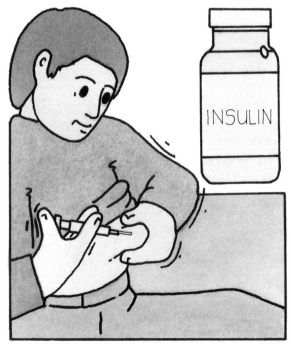

There are operations that people need to make them well. Once upon a time these operations hurt dreadfully because there was no way to stop the pain. Now there are drugs called anaesthetics and analgesics. They stop your body from feeling pain.

So drugs can be used for very good reasons. If they are used carefully, in just the right amount, what they do in your body is good.

But if some of them are used too much, or are used for the wrong reasons, then what they do is bad.

They stop being safe. They are very dangerous drugs.

A lot of people spoil their bodies by using some drugs badly.

The sort of drugs that people use badly are the sort that go to the brain and make strange feelings happen.

Some of them make people very excited.

Some of them make people feel very strong and energetic.

Some of them make people very relaxed.

Some of them make people feel extremely happy.

Some of them make people sleepy.

Some of them make people feel wobbly and dizzy.

Some of them make people forget all the things that worry and upset them.

But all of these drugs are like the chemicals and the alcohol you have already read about in this book.

They make you have bad feelings as well as good ones.

They do bad things inside bodies.

They all make people who use them want more and more, because the good feelings they bring get less and less, and the bad feelings get worse and worse. Just like alcohol, they make people addicted, so that they think they can't live without them.

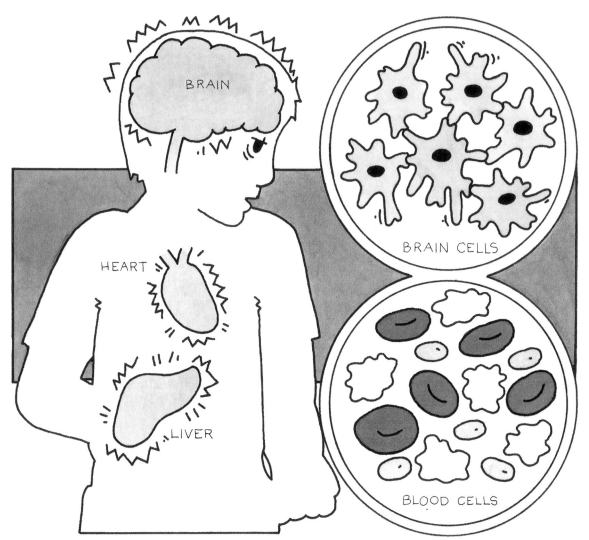

BRAIN

HEART

LIVER

BRAIN CELLS

BLOOD CELLS

They hurt their livers, which have to make the poisonous drugs unpoisonous. They make their eyes red, they make their noses run, they make spots on their faces.

Some people die because of the bad things the drugs do to their bodies.

Because some of these drugs are so dangerous and do so many bad things to people, there are laws about them.

They are not allowed to be bought and sold unless a doctor tells you to take them.

The lawmakers hope this will stop people from using them.

It doesn't.

And then the bad things the drugs do inside people's bodies get worse and worse, as well as the feelings.

What are the bad things the drugs do to people's bodies?

They spoil their brain cells so that their brains stop working as they should.

The person may become mentally ill.

They may damage their hearts so that they can't beat properly anymore.

They may spoil their blood cells so that they can't do their job of carrying oxygen.

We all know that if a thing is wrong and the law says you must not do it, and says you will go to prison if you are caught doing it, then sensible people won't do it.

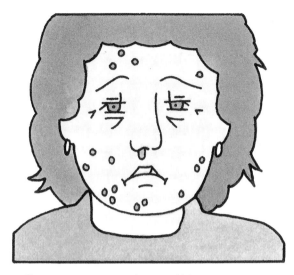

But not everyone is sensible.

And some people say the law is not fair anyway.

They say that tobacco and chemicals and alcohol hurt people too, but the law does not say it is wrong to buy and sell *them*.

So they ignore all the laws.

But many other people say this is wrong. They say that alcohol is not a bad drug if it is used sensibly, so people ought to be allowed to decide for themselves about it.

They say that chemicals are needed for so many different reasons, like painting things and making glue, that it is impossible to make laws about them.

They say that even though everyone knows tobacco is a bad thing, and hurts people, it doesn't hurt them as much as the illegal drugs do, and anyway it has been around for so long it ought to go on being legal.

Others argue with these arguments and say *they* are wrong. They say that some of the illegal drugs are allowed in some parts of the world, so they ought to be allowed everywhere.

It is a very difficult argument and it will take a long time to get everyone to agree about what ought to be done about all the drugs and about tobacco and chemicals and alcohol.

But everyone does agree now that some of the drugs are definitely so dangerous that they must always be illegal.

They are the ones that users get addicted to very, very quickly.

One of the most dangerous is the one called HEROIN.

What is heroin?
It is made from poppies. They have in them a chemical called opium.

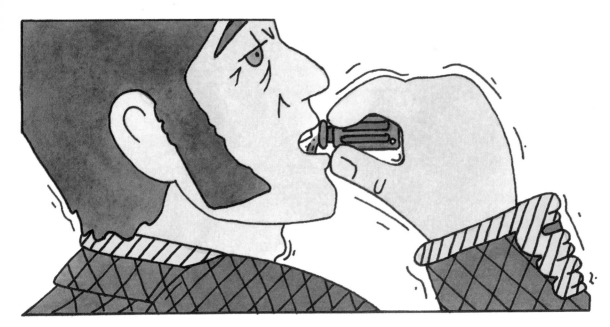

Long ago, in India and in China, people discovered that when they put parts of the poppy in pipes and smoked them, they had strange visions and had strange feelings and their aches and pains went away.

They did not know how dangerous the opium could be if it was used too much, and how it could hurt their bodies, so they grew more and more poppies and encouraged more and more people to smoke them.

And so the use of opium spread everywhere. It was used in medicines with names like LAUDANUM and MORPHIA, and it was also made into a special sort of morphia called heroin.

Doctors used to give it to sick people, to stop their pain, and to make them feel better.

Then they discovered it also made people ill and addicted so they stopped using it. Doctors still use morphia to stop pain, but they use it very, very carefully. They never let their patients use too much.

How do opium and all the drugs made from it help people who hurt and make them feel well?

Inside our brains there are special pieces called receptors. They have a particular shape, and when chemicals that have the same shape reach them, they join together like the pieces of a jigsaw puzzle and make a perfect fit.

When that happens, then the messages that come to the brain from different parts of the body—and which say, "Ouch! I hurt!" can't get through.

So the pain can't be felt.

Also, real messages from the eyes and the ears and the fingers can't get through and

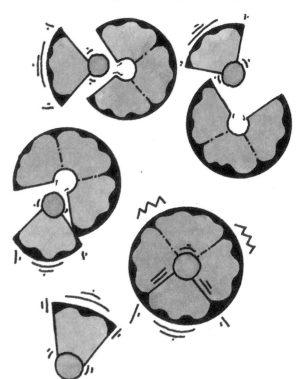

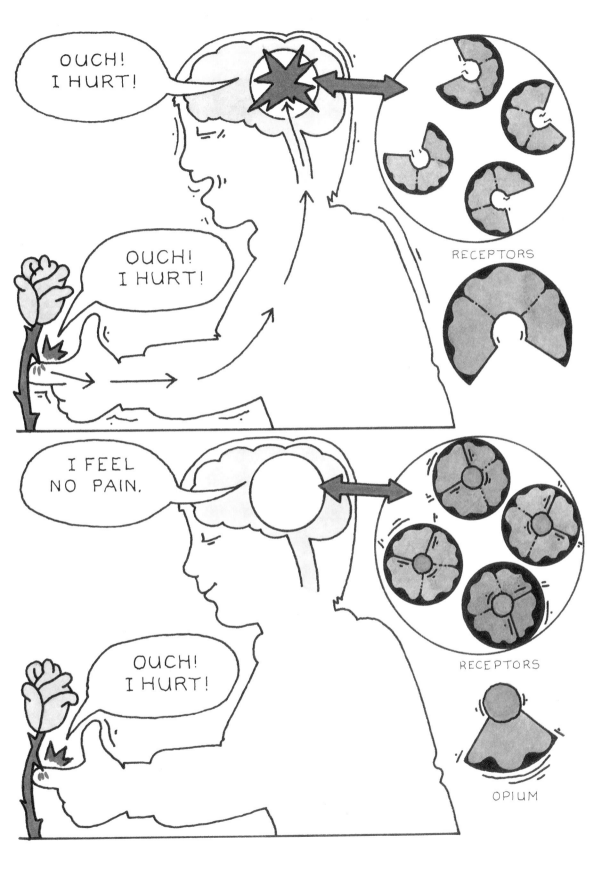

the person "sees" things that aren't there, and "hears" sounds that aren't there, and "feels" touches that aren't there.

It is like having very strong dreams while you are awake. These dreams are called HALLUCINATIONS.

Also a feeling of great happiness comes into the person's mind. They feel that eve-rything is wonderful. This feeling is called EUPHORIA.

But the jigsaw doesn't stay fitted together for long.

Soon after taking the heroin the person finds that the good feeling fades away. The strange dreams stop being interesting and become terrifying instead.

Messages from his body start to reach his brain in a hurtful way. Even an ordinary touch feels like a wallop.

His bones and joints ache.

He feels sick and shaky and frightened.

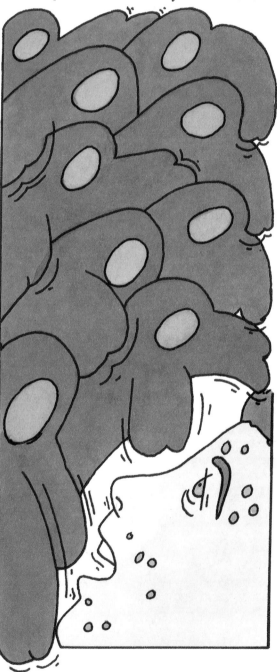

He begins to sweat and that makes him shiver.

That is when he looks for more of the drug to take to help him feel better. And more and more. He is addicted.

The dreadful thing about opium drugs like heroin is that people get addicted to them very, very soon.

A person who drinks too much alcohol may take years to be truly addicted.

A person who uses heroin may become addicted after using it just a few times.

When people are addicted to heroin, that is all they think about. They think about when they last had some and when they are next going to have some.

They can't work or play or do anything but think about heroin.

And because the drug is illegal, they have to think about how to get it. They can't just go to a store! They have to go to people who make them pay a lot of money for it.

They may steal to get that money.

Or hurt other people.

All this is why people who are addicted to heroin are very, very unhappy people.

But that is not all. Because it is so difficult to be an addict, they often stop living in proper homes and go to be with other addicts, and live in the streets or in any corner they can find.

They don't eat enough or wash enough, and so become ill from all the germs they meet every day.

If they inject heroin through needles, as some do, and then don't clean the needles, they catch dreadful illnesses.

Altogether, being a heroin addict is a sick and unhappy person to be.

And though the other drugs that people use may not be quite as bad as heroin, some of them almost are.

Whatever illegal drug it is, it can make people who use it ill and unhappy.

Why do people use drugs like heroin to start with if they know what it does?

Some don't know. (That is why this book was written. So that as many people as possible can know before they meet someone who might invite them to try a dangerous drug.)

Some are conceited people who know, but think they are much too clever to get into any trouble from the drug. They think they can just try it for fun and stop when they like. (They're wrong, of course. No one is that clever.)

Some are very unhappy people who don't have homes and families that make them feel loved and comfortable. So they look for something to take away their bad feelings.

(Drugs don't help. They bring more bad feelings than they ever take away.)

Some are frightened people who want to be like all the other people they know who use drugs. So they do what they do to be loved by them. (They aren't, of course. People who use drugs usually get so unhappy they can't love anyone.)

And for some people, no one knows why.

They are happy people at home and they know they are loved.

They have lots of friends who don't even use drugs—not ever!

They are not silly enough to think they are more clever than other people.

But still they use the drugs and still they get addicted.

It is very sad.

Will you let it happen to you?

How to Keep Your Body Safe

What do you think of the people who spoil their clever bodies in all these different ways we have described?

Do you think they are just silly?
Or you think they are sad?
Some of them are just silly.
All of them are sad.
Some of them become sad after spoiling their bodies.
Some of them are sad before they start spoiling their bodies.
And that is why they start.

Not all the people in the world are happy. If you are happy, you are a lucky person.

But even lucky people who are happy have problems sometimes.
They get frightened.
Or lonely.
Or they think no one likes them.

Most people when they get feelings like this can be patient until something nice happens and the feelings go away.
But for some people, the bad, sad feelings are there all the time.
Maybe they have parents who are unhappy. Unhappy grown ups are not very good at helping their children to be happy.
Maybe things have gone wrong for their families and that makes them unhappy.

Maybe the people they meet at school aren't kind to them.

Maybe they have an illness or a handicap that makes life difficult for them.

Maybe they are angry because of grown ups telling them what to do all the time.

Maybe they are bored.

All these things can make people very unhappy.

So what should people do about unhappy feelings?

THEY SHOULD TALK ABOUT THEM.

The worst thing about unhappy feelings is that they grow in the dark. It is dark inside you, so if you never talk about how you feel, the feelings stay inside, and grow bigger.

So they look for something to take away the unhappy feelings.

Drinking something or breathing in something that makes you go whoozy or sleepy or giggly or gives you a feeling of being happy for a while may seem a good way to get rid of unhappy feelings.

Especially if there are other people doing it with you.

And to start with, maybe it does.

But it doesn't last, does it? Look again at the pages of this book that explain what happens when you use tobacco, alcohol, chemicals, or drugs.

And bigger and bigger and bigger . . . .

Whom should you talk to about unhappy feelings?

Sometimes you can talk to your mother or your father or both.

Sometimes you can talk to your grandmother or grandfather or both.

Sometimes you can talk to aunts and uncles.

And sometimes you can talk to your friends.

Or at school you can talk to a teacher.

Choose the one with the friendliest face, the one you like best, and talk to him or her about all the things that worry you. Teachers are very good at helping people with problems.

But, of course, don't talk to strangers. That can make more problems for you.

Sometimes people spoil their bodies by

using tobacco and alcohol and chemicals and drugs because they want excitement. When you are young, your body is quick and new, and this makes you daring and adventurous. You need to be that way, so that you can learn. Being daring when you are young helps you to be able to become a grown up.

And some young people may get the idea that using these things is daring and adventurous because the feelings they get are so interesting.

Well, maybe they are. But remember, the good feelings don't last.

Is there a way to get those feelings that

won't spoil your body? And which will last?
Yes, there is.

Suppose the feelings you want are the sort that make you dizzy and make you walk about all wobbly, and make everything you look at seem to shiver?

Well, you can get that feeling easily. Try doing twisters, for example. Hold your friend's hands, crossed over, and then, pulling on each other, twist round and round as fast as you can.

This will make your head spin and make you wonderfully whoozy. Only be sure to do it on soft grass, in case you fall over after you let go of your friend's hands! Or try rolling down a soft grassy hill, over and over so that the world swoops all round you. That can feel wonderful. Or try swinging high on a swing. Or going round and round on a merry-go-round.

All these give you the same wonderfully dizzy feelings, but quite safely.

And you can get those feelings any time you want.

Suppose the feeling that you want is to see things that aren't there—to dream strange dreams even though you are awake?

That is very easy. All you have to do is lie down, or sit in a comfortable chair, close your eyes, and tell yourself a story.

Imagine you are in an interesting place where you would like to be.

Like a beautiful beach.

Or high on a mountainside.

Or far into a green forest.

Or deep in a spooky cave.

Look inside your mind at the scenery and wait to see what happens.

If you sit or lie quietly, soon a story will start to happen, there inside your head. You will make up all sorts of pictures, all by yourself.

You don't need drugs to make dreams.

You can make your own.

Suppose the feeling you want is the very, very happy one called euphoria. Is there a way to get that safely?

Yes, there is.

Remember how inside your brain there are specially shaped parts called receptors, which exactly fit the shape of the opium poppy bits?

They are there not just to fit the opium poppy. Nature never makes parts of one sort of thing in this world just to fit parts of another. Nature only makes things inside bodies which fit parts of that body itself.

That means that if there are specially shaped receptors in your brain, there must be somewhere in your body other specially shaped parts made to fit them. And there are. They are a sort of natural chemical your body makes when it is hurt, or is working extra hard.

Have you ever noticed how, when you cut yourself or bruise yourself or bump

44

yourself, at first it feels very sore indeed? And then after a while it stops being so sore?

That is because of the way your body makes this special chemical to stop the hurt. The chemical is poured out into your blood from the place where you were hurt, and goes to your brain. It fits the receptors there and at once the jigsaw pieces join together and make a perfect fit.

And when that happens the message of "Ouch! I hurt!", which is coming from the place that is hurt, can't get through. So the pain can't be felt so much. And the happy feeling called euphoria comes too, because the safe natural chemical in your own clever body makes it happen.

The scientists who discovered this special chemical had to give it a name.

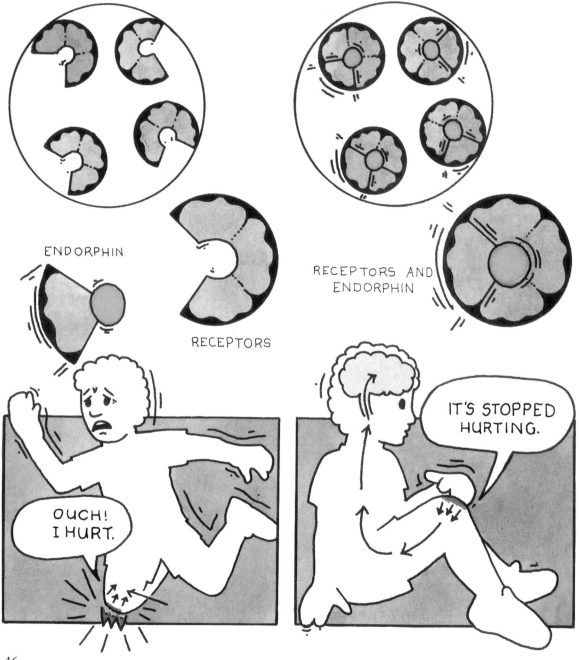

ENDORPHIN

RECEPTORS

RECEPTORS AND ENDORPHIN

OUCH! I HURT.

IT'S STOPPED HURTING.

They called it ENDORPHIN because that means "the morphia inside," and because morphia comes from the opium poppy and is the same shape. But morphia, like heroin, is dangerous. Endorphin is not, because your own body makes it.

You can make lots of the endorphin go to your brain to make you feel happy, if you want to. But you don't have to hurt yourself to do it.

It isn't only hurts that make your body make endorphin. Working your muscles extra hard does too.

So, going for a long hard swim can make you feel very happy and good inside.

Or running about a lot can do it.

Or dancing to bouncy music can do it.

Anything that is hard work for your muscles can make your brain fill up with the

good safe endorphins that your body makes.

47

And the good safe endorphins make your

body feel good and happy.
So there are lots of ways to enjoy exciting feelings and do daring adventurous things without spoiling your body.

Isn't it good that just running and jumping, swimming and dancing can be better than tobacco and alcohol, chemicals and drugs?

Some of the things you have learned about in this book are very sad.
There are some people who think it is better not to tell children about such sad things.

But there are others who think it is better to tell children all they need to know so that they can take good care of themselves.

They think that a child who doesn't know is like a child who is naked in a cold world.

That is why this book was written for you.

To show you how your good body could be spoiled if you didn't know how to take care of it.

Now you know.

Now you can enjoy your clever body properly.